Woody trail

Toilet

Forest

Swimming hole

D1275223

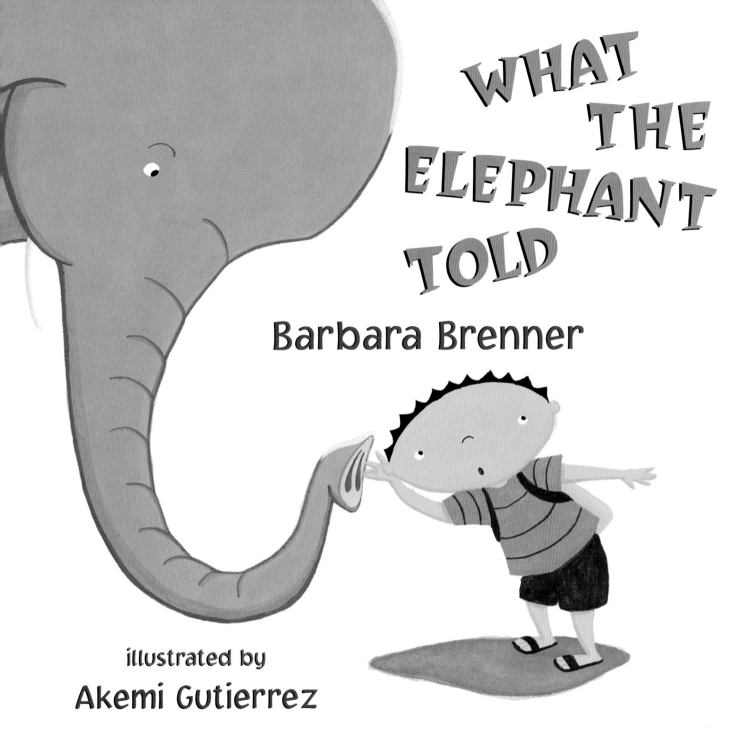

WHAT THE ELEPHANT TOLD

Barbara Brenner

illustrated by

Akemi Gutierrez

Henry Holt and Company • New York

Henry Holt and Company, LLC, Publishers since 1866
115 West 18th Street, New York, New York 10011
www.henryholt.com

Distributed in Canada by H. B. Fenn and Company Ltd.

Library of Congress Cataloging-in-Publication Data
Brenner, Barbara.
What the elephant told / Barbara Brenner; illustrated by Akemi Gutierrez.
Summary: A young boy and a young elephant realize that there are many similarities
between them—they both grew inside their mothers, they both like to play, they hold on
to a grown-up when they are afraid, and they both take naps.
[1. Babies—Fiction. 2. Elephants—Fiction. 3. Animals—Infancy—Fiction.]
I. Gutierrez, Akemi, ill. II. Title.
PZ7.B7518 Wh 2003   [E]—dc21   2002004359

The artist used gouache on Arches watercolor paper to create the illustrations for this book.

ISBN 0-8050-6442-7 / First Edition—2003 / Designed by Martha Rago
Printed in the United States of America on acid-free paper. ∞
1 3 5 7 9 10 8 6 4 2

To Benjamin
—B. B.

For Kathy Lent-Keegan
—A. G.

Once a young boy met a young elephant.
They told each other many things.
And everything they said was true.

"How are elephants born?" the boy asked the elephant.

"Out of our mothers," the elephant answered.

"I was born out of my mother, too," the boy said.
"But first I grew inside her for nine months."

"We grow inside our mothers for twenty-two months," said the elephant.

"I weighed eight pounds when I was born,"
the boy said.

"I weighed two hundred and eight pounds when I was born," the elephant said.

"My mother nursed me when I was a baby," he added.
"Elephant mothers do that."

"My mother nursed me, too," said the boy.

"And when I was full of milk I always gave a little burp."

"When I was full of milk I always gave a great big burp,"
said the elephant.

"I had no teeth when I was born," the boy said.
"I had six," said the elephant. "Two of them
stick out of my mouth. They're tusks."

"What are they for?" asked the boy.

"When they get bigger I'll use them for digging and lifting."

"People use arms for digging and lifting," said the boy.

"Elephants use tusks," said the elephant.

"There's something else I want to ask about,"
the boy said. "Where do elephants pee and poop?"

"In the forest," said the elephant.

"When I was a baby I peed and pooped in my diaper. But I go in the toilet now."

"Elephants never go in the toilet," said the elephant.
"We always go in the forest, even when we grow up."

Now the boy asked, "Who takes care of you?
Do you ever have a baby-sitter?"

"All the grown-up elephants are baby-sitters," the elephant said. "The whole herd helps to take care of me."

"So then you're never afraid of lions
and other wild things?"
"Sometimes I am," said the elephant.

"When I'm afraid I hold a grown-up's hand,"
said the boy.

"When I'm afraid I hold a grown-up's tail,"
said the elephant.

"What do elephants do all day?"
the boy wanted to know.
"We eat grass and bushes and
fruit and mud," said the elephant.

"We play with other elephants.
We take baths and squirt water
on one another with our trunks.
When we get tired we take naps."

"What do you do all day?" asked the elephant.
"I eat and play on the monkey bars and
paint and look at books and watch TV.

When I get tired I take a nap," said the boy.
"Sometimes before I go to sleep I suck my thumb,"
he added.

"Sometimes before I go to sleep I suck my trunk,"
said the elephant.

"I'm sleepy right now," said the boy.

"I am, too," said the elephant.

So they snuggled down on the grass.
And they both had a nice nap.

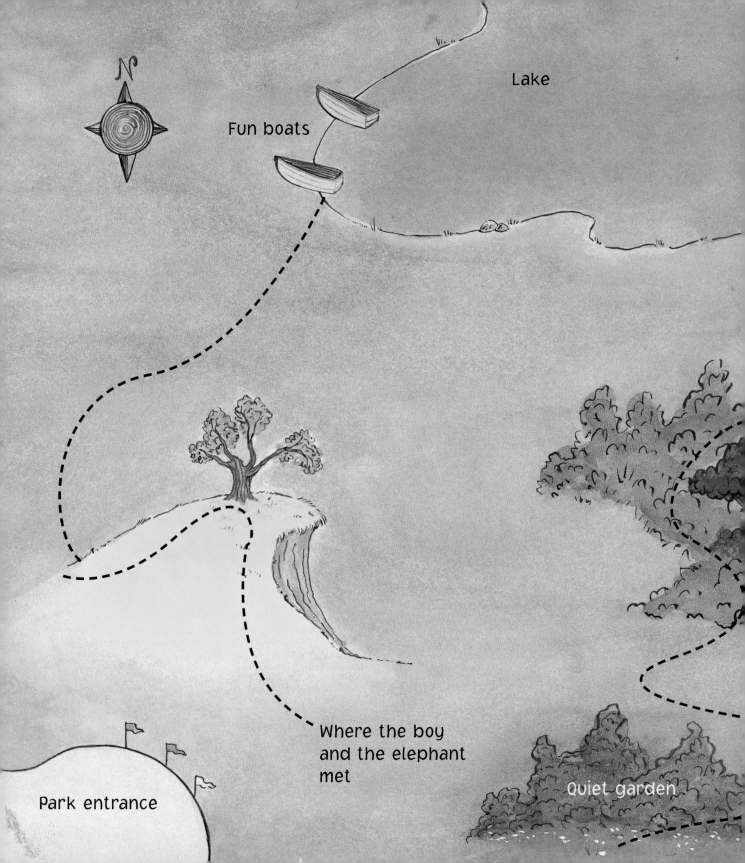